# TRIPLET TROUBLE and the Talent Show Mess

# TRIPLET TROUBLE and the Talent Show Mess

by Debbie Dadey and Marcia Thornton Jones
Illustrated by John Speirs

SCHOLASTIC INC.
New York Toronto London Auckland Sydney

ISBN 0-590-25472-3



12 0/0

Printed in the U.S.A. 40

First Scholastic printing, August 1995

*For the editors at Scholastic who gave us a chance, especially Helen Perelman, Eva Moore, and Diane Molleson.*

*—MTJ and DD*

# Contents

# 1

# Talent Show

Mr. Parker held up a big sign. In big green letters it said TALENT SHOW.

The whole second grade class groaned. I groaned loudest of all. My name is Sam Johnson. I know any time Mr. Parker holds up a sign it means more work.

Alex Tucker waved her hand in the air. "Mr. Parker, Mr. Parker!" she called.

“Can we do whatever we want in the talent show?”

Mr. Parker looked at Alex for a minute. Her short blond hair was sticking straight up on the top of her head. Alex would do anything to be different from her brother and sister.

Alex is one of the Tucker Triplets. Some of the things she does to be different end up getting her into trouble. Terrible trouble.

Mr. Parker rubbed his chin before answering Alex. "You can do anything you want in the talent show. . . ."

"Yes!" Alex yelled, jumping up from her desk.

Mr. Parker went on. "Anything . . . as long as it isn't dangerous and no one gets hurt."

"Oh," Alex said as if she were a balloon that had been popped. She sat down with a sigh. Alex and I have been best friends since kindergarten. I can tell when she is disappointed.

"Now," Mr. Parker said, pointing to the

back of the room. "You may have your snacks and discuss what you want to do for the show."

Ashley Tucker, who looks just like Alex except with long hair, raised her hand. "Oh, Mr. Parker," she called, "shouldn't we wash our hands first?"

Mr. Parker nodded. "Good idea, Ashley."

Alex stuck her tongue out at Ashley. Sometimes I don't know which triplet is worse, Alex or Ashley. Alex is always getting into mischief. But Ashley is always so perfect. Terribly perfect.

Alex took a sticky fruit roll and stuck one end of it in her mouth. The other end hung out like a long purple tongue.

"Sam?" she said to me. Only it sounded more like "Phwam" because her mouth was full of the sticky snack. "What are you doing for the talent show?" she asked.

I shrugged my shoulders and sipped my fruit juice.

Adam Tucker, the third triplet, came up beside me. He had a bag of potato chips. "I want to do a juggling act," he said. "I have a book about juggling." Adam reads a lot of books. He is very smart. Terribly smart.

Ashley tapped him on the shoulder. She had an apple in her hand. "Everyone does juggling. You need to do something really different."

Alex's eyes were shining. "That's what I want to do. Something *really* different."

I looked at Alex and her spiked hair. Whatever she was going to do for the show, I just hoped it wouldn't cause too much trouble!

# 2

# The Big Secret

Alex hunted through Cleo's thick tan fur for fleas. We were sitting on my front porch. Me, Alex, and Cleo. Cleo is my dog. Alex likes Cleo. She's not like her sister, Ashley. When Ashley is around a dog, she gets big red splotches on her face.

I like all the Tucker triplets, but Alex is my best friend. We play ball together and have spitting contests. Sometimes we just sit on my porch. Like today.

Alex found a flea and squinted at it. "Maybe you could use Cleo in your act," Alex said. "She could beg for bones. That's what I'd do for the talent show. If I had a dog." Alex scratched Cleo's ears.

I shrugged. Bones didn't sound very exciting to me. We had been sitting on my front porch ever since school was out. So far, neither of us had come up with a great idea for the talent show.

Alex looked at a worm wiggling across the sidewalk. "I took gymnastics when I was four. Maybe we could do somersaults."

I thought about Alex rolling all over the second grade room. I shook my head.

"We could make a parachute and be daredevils," Alex suggested.

I could see Alex jumping off the school roof with a parachute made out of old socks. I shook my head fast. "You know what Mr. Parker said. It has to be safe."

Just then Adam rode his bike up the

driveway and skidded to a stop. A brown paper bag hung from his handlebars.

"What's in the bag?" Alex asked.

"None of your business," Adam told her.

Alex lifted one of Cleo's floppy ears and squinted. Then she pinched another flea. "If you don't tell me," she said slowly, "I'll put this flea under your pillow."

"I'm not scared of a flea," Adam said. "Besides, you wouldn't dare."

"Yes, I would," Alex said.

There was a long silence. Alex stared at Adam. Adam stared at the flea. And I looked at both of them.

Cleo whined and trotted over to Adam. But she stopped right under his handlebars. Before I could grab her, Cleo bit into

Adam's bag. Shiny red balls spilled out of the sack and bounced all over the sidewalk.

"Balls!" Alex squealed. "Are they for the talent show?"

"For juggling?" I asked.

Adam jumped off his bike and picked up the balls. “I’m not telling. It’s a secret. What are you doing for the show?”

Alex stuck out her chin. “Our act is a secret, too.”

Yeah, I thought. It's such a big secret even I don't know what it is.

"Our act is so good, they'll probably want us to go on TV," Alex bragged.

Adam laughed as he jumped back on his bike. "On TV for the most boring act in the world."

Alex stuck out her tongue as Adam rode away.

# 3

# Card Game

"This is no fun," Alex said. "We've been sitting here half the afternoon trying to think of an act. I'm bored." It was a whole day later and we were sitting on my porch again.

"Me too," I said. "Let's do something else."

Then Alex had a brilliant idea. At least

she thought it was brilliant. I can tell when Alex comes up with one of her ideas. Her eyes get big and round and then she snaps her fingers right in front of her nose. "I've got it!" she said. "We could play cards!"

Alex always wins when we play cards. Mostly because she makes up her own rules. "It's no fun with just two people," I told her.

“Then we’ll get Adam and Ashley to play.” Alex hopped off the porch. I had to hurry to catch up.

The triplets live five houses away from me, but their house and yard don’t look like mine. My dad planted yellow and pink flowers around our two big trees. But Alex’s yard looks like it sprouted bicycles, soccer balls, and jump ropes. I guess when there are triplets, having a neat yard is just too hard.

Alex let the screen door slam before yelling for Ashley and Adam. They both galloped down the steps. They must have been bored too, because they thought playing cards was a great idea. But I wasn’t so sure. Especially when Alex started winning. She didn't just win one or two games. She won every single game.

"You're cheating," Adam said.

"Am not," Alex told him.

"Yes, you are." Ashley stood up and put her hands on her hips. "I'm going to tell on you."

Alex stuck out her chin. Ashley's face turned red. I knew what would happen next. When Ashley tattled, there was trouble.

Ashley ran upstairs to Mrs. Tucker's office. Mrs. Tucker is a writer and spends a lot of time in her office tapping away on a computer.

She clomped down the steps and stopped in front of Alex. Mrs. Tucker looked as tall as a giant and a whole lot meaner.

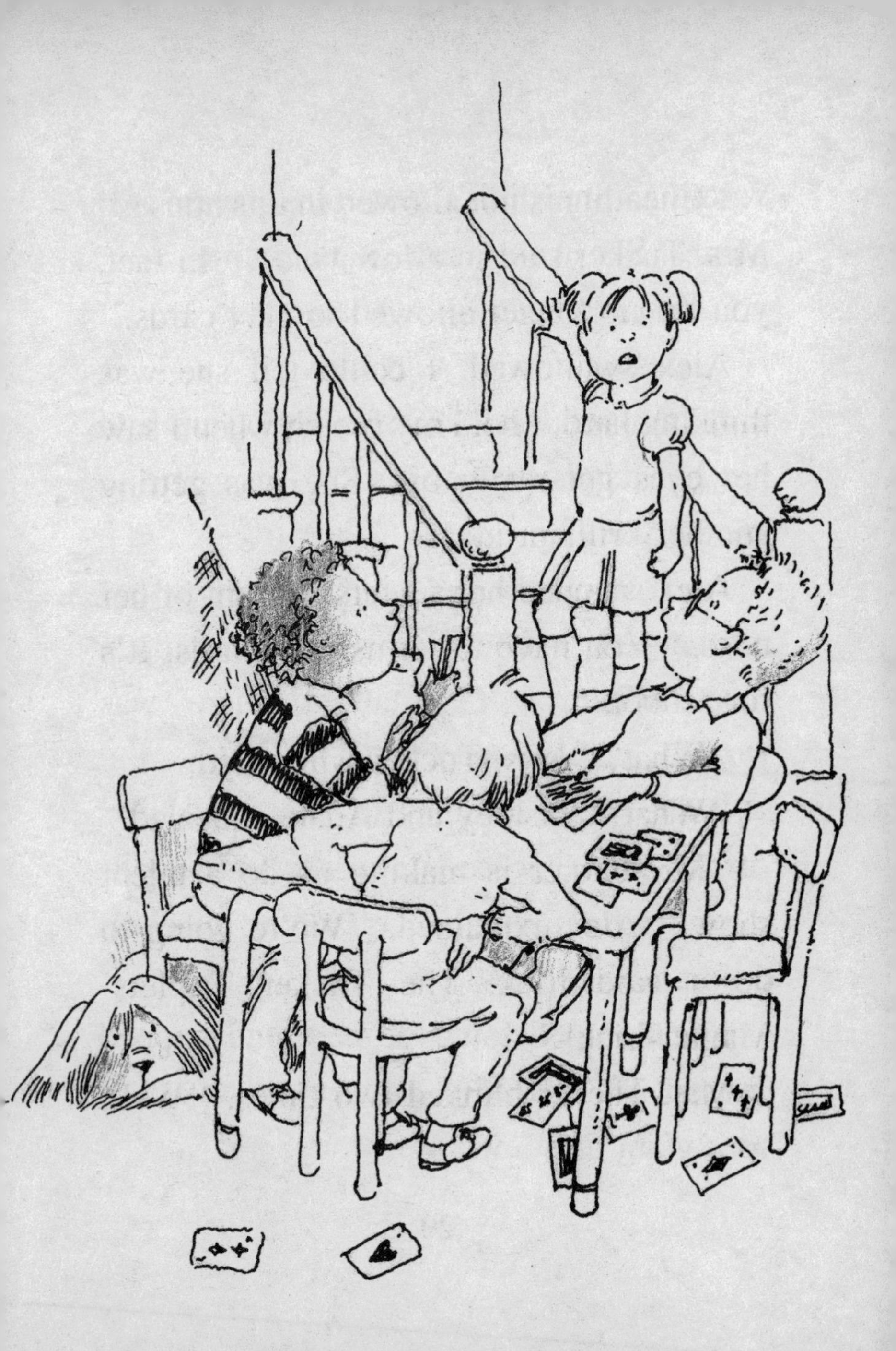

"Cheating is not allowed in this house," Mrs. Tucker said in a low voice. "In fact, you are no longer allowed to play cards."

Alex swallowed. I could tell she was thinking hard. I held my breath when I saw her eyes get really big. She was getting another brilliant idea.

Alex snapped her fingers in front of her nose. "You have to let us play cards. It's for school."

"What?" Mrs. Tucker whispered.

"What?" Ashley and Adam squealed.

"Mr. Parker is making us do a talent show," Alex explained. "We're going to do a card trick. The Tucker Triplets' Magic Trick!"

Mrs. Tucker blinked two times. "Well,

I'm glad you three are working together for a change.''

Adam gulped. Ashley stood there with her mouth hanging open.

I closed my eyes. This was the worst brilliant idea Alex had ever had. Nobody made a sound. Sometimes quiet is good. But not when the triplets are around. This kind of quiet sounded like trouble. Triplet trouble!

# 4

# Dirty Trick

"That was a dirty trick!" Adam yelled after his mother left. "I wanted to do a juggling act."

"And I wanted to do ballet," Ashley said, looking like she was going to cry.

Alex put her hand on Ashley's shoulder. "Juggling and ballet are okay, but magic is special."

Adam didn't believe Alex. He folded his arms and stared at her. "What kind of magic trick can we do with cards?"

"We can do anything. The trick doesn't have to be with cards." Alex smiled. "We could cut Ashley in half and then try to put her back together."

"No way," Ashley yelled. "I'm telling Mom!"

"Don't worry, I saw a trick on TV. Wait here." Alex ran into the kitchen. In a minute she was back with a jug of milk and a big piece of paper.

"Watch this!" Alex twisted the paper into a cone.

"It looks like an ice cream cone," Adam said. "What are you going to do with that?"

“It’s a magic cone,” Alex told us. “The milk will disappear.” Then, before our eyes, she poured the milk into the cone. But the milk didn’t disappear. It splashed all over the floor.

"Oh, no—I guess I didn't say the magic words."

"It's a magic mess!" Ashley squealed. "I'm definitely telling Mom."

Alex grabbed Ashley's arm. "Don't worry, there are lots of other things we could do." Then Alex looked at me and I knew I was in trouble.

“We could make Sam disappear,” Alex said. She smiled and showed the space where her tooth used to be.

“Don’t look at me,” I told her. “I have my own act for the talent show.”

I thought this might be a good time to leave. As the screen door shut behind me I could hear the triplets yelling. I knew one thing. The Tucker Triplets’ Magic Trick was definitely going to be trouble.

# 5

# Sam's Act

It was nice and quiet at home. At least it was until I started practicing my act. I dusted off Dad's old saxophone.

I blew into the saxophone and made music. I thought it was music. But Cleo wasn't so sure. That's why she started howling. I blew and Cleo howled.

We were so loud I couldn't tell if we were good or not. I needed to find out. That's why I headed back over to the triplets' house.

I wanted help, but all I found was a mess. A triplet mess.

Cards were scattered all over the Tuckers' basement. Ashley had red, blue, and yellow scarves twisted all around her.

Alex and Adam were standing in front of a table with a big black hat. "Try it again," Alex told Adam.

"I could do it a million times," Adam said, shaking his head. "I can't pull anything out of this hat."

"You're just not trying hard enough," Alex told him.

"How about this for hard enough?" Adam bopped the tall hat on Alex's head. "I'm not doing a dumb magic trick," he hollered and stomped up the stairs.

“You can have these silly scarves. I’m doing my own act, too!” Ashley threw the scarves at Alex and ran up the stairs.

Alex pulled off the scarves and top hat. She looked at me. "I guess the great Tucker Triplets' Magic Trick is going to be harder than I thought."

## 6

# The Best Act of All

A week later, Mr. Parker held up a sign. In big purple letters it said TALENT SHOW PRACTICE.

A few kids clapped. Somebody groaned. I think it was Alex. Some kids grabbed their props. A few kids ran to put on costumes.

Mr. Parker called Randy first. Randy

juggled three beanbags in the air. He only dropped them five times.

Then Barbara skipped and hopped and turned circles until she got dizzy. She called it ballet.

Bobby did a handstand against the wall. He left two big shoe prints right beside the classroom door.

Maria twirled a silver baton around and around. Mr. Parker didn't say a word when she knocked the pencil can off his desk.

I lugged Dad's saxophone to the front of the room and blew as hard as I could. I think my act was the best. It was definitely the loudest.

Everyone had an act. Everybody, that is, but the triplets. When it was their turn, nobody moved. Not Adam. Not Ashley. Even Alex was completely still. Mr. Parker likes it when the classroom is still. But not that kind of still.

Mr. Parker cleared his throat while we waited. Adam looked at Ashley. Ashley stared at Alex. Alex glared at Adam.

Randy whispered, "It's your turn."

"The triplets aren't ready," Barbara said.

I saw Alex's eyes get big and round.

Maria pointed her baton at Alex. "I bet they don't even have an act."

Alex snapped her fingers in front of her nose. I held my breath. I knew trouble wasn't far away. I was right.

"We do too have an act," Alex said. Her smile showed where her front tooth was missing. "We have the best act of all."

"We'd like to see it," Mr. Parker said.

Alex shook her head. "We can't show it to you. That would give it away. You'll just have to wait until the talent show to see the famous Tucker Triplets' Magic Trick."

# 7

# Magic Toys

"Now you've done it," Adam snapped.

"We *have* to do an act with you," Ashley said. "Thanks to your big mouth."

It was after school and we were walking home. Well, I was walking. Adam stomped. Ashley clomped. And Alex skipped.

"You should be glad I'm letting you in

on my act,'' Alex told them, ''since you don't have acts of your own.''

''I did,'' Adam said. ''I was going to juggle until Randy did his act.''

Ashley crossed her arms. ''I was going to do ballet, but Barbara did her dance first.''

''So that leaves magic,'' Alex said with a grin. ''And I have the perfect plan.''

I am used to Alex's plans. She has lots of them. The only thing they're perfect at is trouble. But there is one thing about Alex's plans. They're always fun to watch. I followed the triplets home just to see what would happen.

Alex led us to the basement. A huge pile of broken toys lay in the corner. Alex dug in and pulled out half of a baton.

"Maria is twirling a baton," Ashley reminded her.

"This isn't just any old baton," Alex whispered like she was telling a secret. "This is a magic wand!"

"That isn't a magic wand," Adam said. "It's a broken stick and I don't want to have anything to do with it or your stupid magic tricks!"

"Fine." Alex crossed her arms. "You come up with an act."

Usually I like it when the triplets come up with ideas. But not when they're mad. Then there's trouble. I sat down on the basement steps to watch.

"I know the perfect magic act," Ashley said. "We can make flowers appear out of a hat."

"That didn't work with the rabbit," Adam said, shaking his head. "We should do card tricks. There's a book at the library I could use."

"I don't want to do that," Ashley whined.

"You could tie me up and then I could escape, like the great Harry Houdini," Alex suggested.

"No!" Ashley and Adam shouted together. I shook my head and went home. It looked like the Tucker Triplets' Magic Trick was in big trouble. Maybe working together is just too hard for triplets.

# 8

# The Show

Mr. Parker held up a sign. In big red letters it said WELCOME TO THE TALENT SHOW. Our classroom was filled with parents. My dad sat in front, next to Mrs. Tucker.

Mr. Parker cleared his throat and asked Randy to go first. Randy juggled. He only dropped his beanbags two times. When he was finished everyone clapped.

After Maria twirled her baton it was my turn. I gulped and carried Dad's saxophone to the front of the room. Everyone stared at me. I mean they were *really* staring. I almost ran out of the room.

Then I saw Alex. She smiled at me, showing the empty space where her tooth used to be. I smiled back at her and started to blow.

I blew louder than ever before. Everyone clapped when I was done and Alex slapped me on the back. Sometimes Alex is a terribly good friend.

Everyone in the class did their act. It took a long time, but finally only the triplets were left. I held my breath when Mr. Parker looked at them. Alex didn't move. Ashley

didn't move. Adam didn't move.

What would Mr. Parker do to them? Would they get into terrible trouble?

Mr. Parker cleared his throat. "Alex, Adam, and Ashley," he said, "are you ready?"

Suddenly Alex smiled and snapped her fingers in front of her nose. "The Tucker Triplets are always ready!"

Everything happened at once. Ashley pushed a button on a tape player and loud music blasted throughout the room. Ashley bounced up and twirled around in front of the chalkboard with red, green, blue, and yellow scarves. Adam raced around the room, juggling balls.

Alex put on a long black coat and held up a huge, empty black hat for us to see.

"Ladies and gentlemen," Alex yelled. "The Tucker Triplets will now amaze you with their disappearing act. First, the scarves."

Ashley danced around and dropped her scarves into the hat.

"And now, the balls," Alex called. Adam dropped one, two, three balls into the hat.

"And now, the Tucker Triplets' Magic Wand!" Alex pointed to the back of the room.

Everyone watched as Adam and Ashley ran to the back of the room. They opened a shiny box and lifted out the broken baton. Only now it was covered with sparkles, and bright streamers dangled from the ends. It really looked like a magic wand.

Adam and Ashley carried the wand to the front of the room. Alex took it and waved it over the hat. "*Ala . . . kazam . . . ala . . . kazoom . . . Triplet Power. Kaboom!*"

When Alex held up the hat it was empty. I gasped and everyone clapped, even Mr. Parker. My dad and Mrs. Tucker cheered.

"How did you do that?" I asked.

Alex just smiled, showing the space where her front tooth used to be. "Magicians stick together," she said. "We can't tell our magic secrets."

Then Adam, Alex, and Ashley held hands and bowed.

I guess sometimes being a triplet isn't so terrible. Sometimes being a triplet is terrific.